William Watson

The Year of Shame

Poems

William Watson

The Year of Shame
Poems

ISBN/EAN: 9783337206833

Printed in Europe, USA, Canada, Australia, Japan

Cover: Foto ©Andreas Hilbeck / pixelio.de

More available books at **www.hansebooks.com**

THE YEAR OF SHAME

BY

WILLIAM WATSON

WITH AN INTRODUCTION

BY

THE BISHOP OF HEREFORD

JOHN LANE

THE BODLEY HEAD

LONDON AND NEW YORK

1897

Press of J. J. Little & Co.
Astor Place, New York

CONTENTS

INTRODUCTION

THE words of a true poet, like a Greek statue, need no framework or drapery. They tell their own tale, and we prefer to read them without note, or comment, or introduction, or supplement; because it is universally true that deep answereth to deep in human hearts.

But this little volume goes out, as I understand, on the present occasion, not only as a poet's impassioned utterance, but still more as a patriotic appeal, intended to provoke men to serious thought about national honour and duty, and to move the fountains of charity on behalf of those sufferers who, having endured long agony and sore bereavement, and horrors that cannot be plainly described, are now perishing in misery and want amidst all the cruel rigour of an Armenian winter, whilst the Pharaohs of modern Christendom harden their hearts against their bitter cry.

Such is my apology for this brief introduction, written because it has been felt that a few words of plain prose may assist in carrying the book into some homes which it would not otherwise have entered.

If so, my modest and humble share in the matter will have served its purpose, and will be abundantly justified.

Some readers of the poet's passionate outpourings, as they sit in their safe and undefiled English homes, may possibly feel that one and another of his burning utterances are hard sayings which they cannot endorse or approve, and it may be fully acknowledged that most of us, and not least the poet himself, would desire in due place to give full weight to every extenuating circumstance; but when duty seems to be calling to deaf ears, and when statesmen seem to be afflicted with moral paralysis, it is hardly the moment for extenuation, and even if the historian extenuates he will not acquit us.

If these poems could be edited and illustrated with all the lurid picture of the recurring abominations and infamies that set the writer's heart aflame in each case, if every reader could see the pandemonium of lust and cruelty, as he saw it, with its background of unfulfilled and disregarded moral obligations on our part, and of cynical callousness and intrigue on the part of selfish monarchs and diplomatists, who call themselves Christians, what may seem at first

sight to be the language of exaggeration, or
the cry of an over-sensitive spirit, would be
felt to be the plain words of truth and sober-
ness. At all events, when we have made
every possible deduction for the intensity of
poetic feeling, more highly strung, no doubt,
and more finely touched than that of common men, there remains in these poems the
unmistakeable voice of genuine native English patriotism and humanity, nursed on
the record of English story, and inspired by
our inheritance of honour and duty, as dis-
tinct from the pinchbeck patriotism of the
commercial jingo, who is unhappily becoming very prominent in English life, and is
very militant, if any material interests are
threatened, but all for peace and patience
and concerted action, when the only thing
concerned is a question of old-fashioned
honour and moral obligation.

To those who are possessed by this spirit, and look upon international duty as something that is to be measured chiefly, if not entirely, by financial and material interests, these poems can hardly be welcome or attractive reading. On the other hand, multitudes of plain English folk of every degree, saddened and humiliated by a spectacle which looks so very like the lowering of the flag of English chivalry at the secret dictates of the bondholder and commercial speculator, are beginning to feel that our country greatly needs such moral tonics as that which is furnished by these searching and stirring poems.

We were told not long since by a distinguished historian, in language which has been quoted with much approval, that the traditional and characteristic policy of Englishmen, to which more than anything else our country owes its high place among the nations, has been their habit of going their own way, following their own sense of duty, and guarding their own honour, " uncaring consequences " ; but it is impossible to read the history of our share in Turkish affairs during the last two years, and our long-continued acquiescence in Turkish barbarities—an altogether ignoble acquiescence when set side by side with our undertakings and obligations—without feeling that this proud and independent spirit seems to be in danger of dying out ; and these poems will do a great service to England if they compel men to think of the ominous change thus suggested, and to study the inner and true meaning of such a change.

We are very loth to believe that our statesmen, affected by this insidious influence, and involved in the enervating atmosphere of

Continental diplomacy, have lost their nerve and resource, and yet this idea is spreading in men's minds, as they wait in weariness of heart through the long months and seasons, which are fruitful in nothing but fresh insolence and massacre.

We are willing to admit that they have opposed to them at least two tremendous forces, which make the situation very difficult; but such occasions are the brave and strong man's opportunity, and he turns them into those moments of noble action, which are the leaven of his country's greatness. But, as yet, we look in vain for the signs of this ennobling strength. Our statesmen seem to be overawed on the one hand by the demoralising influence of the financier, the bondholder, and the speculator, an influence which threatens to become as disastrous in modern Christendom as it was in ancient

Rome, and on the other hand by those great military empires which have strangled the conscience of Europe.

"How much is a man better than a sheep?" said the Divine Word long ago; but our modern diplomacy seems to say the very opposite, as it sits guarding material interests and leaves a helpless and innocent people to perish in slow agony, miserably and unspeakably. The burden of a vast empire is laid upon us—such is the plea—and our first duty is to safeguard our own possessions and all our manifold and ever-growing interests. We are so hard- pressed by financial and other obligations that we dare not run the risk of stepping apart or acting alone, though it was alone that we made our promises on behalf of this forsaken people in the days of the Cyprus Convention.

In answer to all this line of argument,

multitudes of silent Englishmen have been asking, and will continue to ask with growing indignation and sternness, what meanwhile is becoming of English honour, and chivalry, and independence, and sensitive regard for moral obligations; and such men are grateful to a poet who gives voice to this higher and nobler national feeling, because they believe it to be as true for us to-day as it was when Shakespeare wrote the words that

" Where great additions swell and virtue none
It is a dropsied honour."

But, rejoin the diplomatists, in exculpation of their failure, confronted as we are by the vast military organisations of the Continent, our only hope is to hold on to the concert of Europe, whatever betide ; and this notwithstanding their admiration of those makers of England whose proud characteristic it was to go their own way. Had these diplomatists lived in Jerusalem in the days of Hezekiah, they would doubtless have urged with equal emphasis that it was folly in Israel to have the hardihood to stand aloof from the concert of Asia as represented by Sennacherib, and they would have had a very poor opinion of the prophet Isaiah.

Yet it was the prophet who saved the nation and added a new lustre to the name of his people. And it is the spirit of Isaiah that is represented in this book of poems, warning us that the Lord's arm is not shortened, and making us feel that behind those desolated Armenian homes, those tortured and murdered men, those dishonoured and heart-broken women, there stands the vision of a stern and unavoidable reckoning for those who might have saved and would not or dared not.

But it is not our part to apportion the blame. To every one according to his guilt I will repay, saith the Lord, whether it be Tsar, or Emperor, or statesman, or financier, who bars the way.

Those who believe in Christ as the great life of love and sacrifice that came on earth to save the perishing and to comfort the mourner will not fail at this Christmas season to offer up their prayers and to send some gift on behalf of the sufferers who still survive.

Sunt lacrimæ rerum, et mentem mortalia tangunt.

Some who read these lines will be gathering in happy homes—fathers, mothers, sons, and daughters—for a joyful Christmas meeting, others will be saddened as they look on the vacant chair of some loved one; but whether they meet in joy or sorrow, what a contrast is furnished by those Christian households

2

in Armenia, some waiting in helpless and hope-
less dread for the threatened onslaught of
plunder, lust, and butchery, others fatherless
and brotherless, every surviving child an or-
phan, and every woman ravished and defiled.

It is for such as these, left in cold and
hunger and shame and nakedness, that the
appeal comes to us through all the sound of
Christmas bells; and it is the voice of the
Incarnate Christ Himself that is thus calling,
and to those who answer the call His reward
is that which He promised from the beginning, the blessing of the Father.

"I was an hungered and ye gave Me meat;
naked and ye clothed Me; I was sick and ye
visited Me; I was in prison and ye came unto
Me. Inasmuch as ye did it to these desolate
and forsaken ones ye did it unto Me."

J. HEREFORD.

December, 1896.

AUTHOR'S NOTE

THE sonnets and other poems in this book, though they have a certain chronological sequence in point of subject-matter and occasion, are not otherwise meant to be understood as a series.

Sixteen of the sonnets are here reprinted — in some cases with alteration — from my pamphlet, " The Purple East." The remaining pieces have not appeared before, except in newspapers.

I retain, in the sonnet to the Sultan, the inaccurate use of " Abdul," upon which some critics have very naturally commented.

W. W.

I

TO A LADY

DAUGHTER of Ireland,—nay, 'twere better
    said,
Daughter of Ireland's beauty, Ireland's grace,
Child of her charm, of her romance; whose
    face
Is legendary with her glories fled!
The shadow of her living griefs and dead
I pray you to put by a little space,

And mourn with me an ancient Orient race
Outcast and doomed and disinherited.

Though Wrong be strong, though thrones be built on crimes,
To know you, Lady, is to doubt no more
That in the world are mightier powers than these ;
That heaven, the ocean, gains on earth, the shore ;
And that deformity and hate are Time's,
And love and loveliness Eternity's.

THE TURK IN ARMENIA

WHAT profits it, O England, to prevail

In arts and arms, and mighty realms subdue,

And ocean with thine argosies bestrew,

And wrest thy tribute from each golden gale,

If idly thou must hearken to the wail

Of women martyred by the turbaned crew

Whose tenderest mercy was the sword that
  slew,

And hazard not the dinting of thy mail?

We deemed of old thou held'st a charge
  from Him

Who sits companioned by His seraphim,

To smite the wronger with thy destined rod.

Wait'st thou His sign?   Enough, the un-
answered cry

Of virgin souls for vengeance, and on high

The gathering blackness of the frown of
God!

III

IGNOBLE EASE

NEVER henceforth, O England, nevermore
Prate thou of generous effort, righteous aim,
Whose shame is that thou knowest not thy
  shame!
Summer hath passed, and Autumn's thresh-
  ing-floor
Been winnowed; Winter at Armenia's door
Snarls like a wolf; and still the sword and
  flame
Sleep not; *thou only* sleepest; and the same
Cry unto heaven ascends as heretofore;

And the red stream thou might'st have
staunched, yet runs:

And roused by no divinely beckoning
Wraith,

Stirred by no clarion blowing loud and
wide,

Lost in ignoble ease, behold thy sons,

Sitting among the shards of broken faith,

And by the ruins of forgotten pride.

THE PRICE OF PRESTIGE

You in high places; you that drive the
  steeds
Of Empire; you that say unto our hosts,
"Go thither," and they go; and from our
  coasts
Bid sail the squadrons, and they sail, their
  deeds
Shaking the world: lo! from a land that
  pleads
For mercy where no mercy is, the ghosts
Look in upon you faltering at your posts—

Upbraid you parleying while a People
    bleeds

To death.   What stays the thunder in your
    hand?

A fear for England? Can her pillared fame

Only on faith forsworn securely stand,

On faith forsworn that murders babes and
    men?

Are such the terms of Glory's tenure? Then

Fall her accursed greatness, in God's name!

V

HOW LONG?

HEAPED in their ghastly graves they lie, the breeze

Sickening o'er fields where others vainly wait

For burial: and the butchers keep high state

In silken palaces of perfumed ease.

The panther of the desert, matched with these,

Is pitiful; beside their lust and hate,

Fire and the plague-wind are compassionate,

And soft the fang'd lips of the ravening seas.

How long shall they be borne? Is not the
    cup

Of crime yet full? Doth devildom still lack

Some consummating crown, that we hold
    back

The scourge, and in Christ's borders give
    them room?

How long shall they be borne, O England?
    Up,

Tempest of God, and sweep them to their
    doom!

VI

REPUDIATED RESPONSIBILITY

I HAD not thought to hear it voiced so plain,
Uttered so forthright, on their lips who
    steer
This nation's course: I had not thought to
    hear
That word re-echoed by an English thane,
Guilt's maiden-speech when first a man lay
    slain,
" Am I my brother's keeper?" Yet full near
It sounded, and the syllables rang clear
As the immortal rhetoric of Cain.

" Wherefore should *we*, sirs, more than they

—or they—

Unto these helpless reach a hand to save?"

An English thane, in this our English air,

Speaking for England? Then indeed her day

Slopes to its twilight, and, for Honour, there

Is needed but a requiem, and a grave.

VII

A HURRIED FUNERAL

A LITTLE deeper, sexton. You forget,

She you would bury 'neath so thin a crust

Of loam, was fiery-souled, and ev'n in dust

She may lie restless, she may toss and fret,

Nay, she might break a seal too lightly set,

And vex, unmannerly, our ease! She must

Beneath no lack of English earth lie thrust,

Would we unhaunted sleep! Nay, deeper

    yet.

Quick, friend, the cortège comes. There—

    that will serve ;

Deep enough now ; and thou'lt need all thy
    nerve,

If, in her coffin, at the last, amid   .

The mourners in the customary suits,

And to the scandal of these decent mutes,

This corpse of England's Honour burst the
    lid !

VIII

ENGLAND TO AMERICA

O TOWERING daughter, Titan of the West,

Behind a thousand leagues of foam secure;

Thou toward whom our inmost heart is pure

Of ill intent: although thou threatenest

With most unfilial hand thy mother's breast,

Not for one breathing-space may Earth
    endure

The thought of War's intolerable cure

For such vague pains as vex to-day thy rest!

But if thou hast more strength than thou
    canst spend

In tasks of Peace, and find'st her yoke too
    tame,

Help us to smite the cruel, to befriend

The succourless, and put the false to shame.

So shall the ages laud thee, and thy name

Be lovely among nations to the end.

IX

A BIRTHDAY

IT is the birthday of the Prince of Peace :

Full long ago He lay with steeds in stall,

And universal Nature knew through all

Her borders that the reign of Pan must

cease.

The fatness of the land, the earth's increase,

Cumbers the board ; the holly hangs in hall;

Somewhat of her abundance Wealth lets

fall ;

It is the birthday of the Prince of Peace.

The dead rot by the wayside ; the unblest

Who live, in caves and desert mountains
lurk

Trembling, His foldless flock, shorn of their
fleece.

Women in travail, babes that suck the
breast,

Are spared not. Famine hurries to her
work.

It is the birthday of the Prince of Peace.

X

THE TIRED LION

SPEAK once again, with that great note of
  thine,

Hero withdrawn from Senates and their
  sound

Unto thy home by Cambria's northern
  bound,

Speak once again, and wake a world supine.

Not always, not in all things, was it mine

To follow where thou led'st: but who hath
  found

Another man so shod with fire, so crowned

With thunder, and so armed with wrath
    divine?

Lift up thy voice once more! The nation's
    heart

Is cold as Anatolia's mountain snows.

Oh, from these alien paths of base repose

Call back thy England, ere thou too depart—

Ere, on some secret mission, thou too start

With silent footsteps, whither no man knows.

XI

THE BARD-IN-WAITING

TREACHERY'S apologist, whose numbers
  rung,
But yesterday, remonstrant in my ear;
Thou to whom England seems a mistress
  dear,
Insatiable of honey from thy tongue:
Because I crouch not fawning slaves among,
How is my service proved the less sincere?
Have not I also deemed her without peer?
Her beauty have not I too seen and sung?
But for the love I bore her lofty ways,

What were to me her stumblings and her
  slips?

And lovely is she still, her maiden lips

Pressed to the lips whose foam around her
  plays!

But on her brow's benignant star whose
  rays

Lit them that sat in darkness, lo! the
  eclipse.

XII

LEISURED JUSTICE

"SHE bides her hour."   And must I then
  believe
That when the day of peril is o'erpast,
She who was great because so oft she cast
All thought of peril to the waves that heave
Against her feet, shall greatly undeceive
Her purblind son who dreamed she shrank
  aghast
From Duty's signal, and shall act at last,
When there is naught remaining to retrieve?
At last! when the last altar is defiled,

And there are no more maidens to deflower—

When the last mother folds with famished
arms

To her dead bosom her last butchered
child—

Then shall our England, throned beyond
alarms,

Rise in her might! Till then, "she bides
her hour."

XIII

THE PLAGUE OF APATHY

THE dewfall of compassion, is it o'er

So soon? So soon is dead indifference
come?

From wintry sea to sea the land lies numb.

With palsy of the spirit stricken sore,

The land lies numb from iron shore to
shore.

The unconcerned, they flourish: loud are
some,

And without shame. The multitude stand
dumb.

The England that we vaunted is no more.

Only the witling's sneer, the worldling's
smile,

The weakling's tremors, fail him not who
fain

Would rouse to noble deed. And all the
while,

A homeless people, in their mortal pain,

Toward one far and famous ocean isle

Stretch hands of prayer, and stretch those
hands in vain.

XIV

THE KNELL OF CHIVALRY

O VANISHED morn of crimson and of gold,

O youth of roselight and romance, wherein

I read of paynim and of paladin,

And Beauty snatched from ogre's dungeoned
　　hold !

Ever the recreant would in dust be rolled,

Ever the true knight in the joust would
　　win,

Ever the scaly shape of monstrous Sin

At last lie vanquished, fold on writhing fold.

Was it all false, that world of princely deeds,

The splendid quest, the good fight ringing

> clear?

Yonder the Dragon ramps with fiery gorge,

Yonder the victim faints and gasps and

> bleeds;

But in his merry England our St. George

Sleeps a base sleep beside his idle spear.

XV

TO RUSSIA

RUSSIA that wast the opener of the door

Through which the captive peoples went

    forth freed;

How art thou changed and fall'n, who giv'st

    no heed

Though in the dust a nation stricken sore

Dies at thy feet; though the red torrents pour

Continual, and to stay them does but need

Thy whisper, thy " Enough!" O fall'n

    indeed,

Russia the Liberator now no more!

4

Hear thou a parable. A savage hound

Did rend a babe; and one that with a word

Or gesture could have called the brute to
heel,

Stood watching; and behold he never stirred

A finger, and his lips vouchsafed no sound.

Shall hound or man God's heaviest judgment
feel?

XVI

A TRIAL OF ORTHODOXY

THE clinging children at their mother's knee
Slain; and the sire and kindred one by one
Flayed or hewn piecemeal; and things
    nameless done,
Not to be told: while imperturbably
The nations gaze, where Rhine unto the sea,
Where Seine and Danube, Thames and
    Tiber run,
And where great armies glitter in the sun,
And great kings rule, and man is boasted
    free !

What wonder if yon torn and naked throng

Should doubt a Heaven that seems to wink
and nod,

And having moaned at noontide, " Lord,
how long?"

Should cry, " Where hidest Thou?" at even-
fall,

At midnight, " Is He deaf and blind, our
God?"

And ere day dawn, " Is He indeed at all?"

XVII

"IF"

YEA, if ye could not, though ye would, lift
 ˈand—
Ye halting leaders—to abridge Hell's reign;
If, for some cause ye may not yet make
 plain,
Yearning to strike, ye stood as one may
 stand
Who in a nightmare sees a murder planned
And hurrying to its issue, and though fain
To stay the knife, and fearless, must
 remain

Madly inert, held fast by ghostly band ;—

If such your plight, most hapless ye of
men !

But if ye could and would not, oh, what
plea,

Think ye, shall stead you at your trial,
when

The thunder-cloud of witnesses shall loom,

With Ravished Childhood on the seat of
doom,

At the Assizes of Eternity ?

XVIII

A WONDROUS LIKENESS

STILL, on Life's loom, the infernal warp and
  weft
Woven each hour! Still, in august renown,
A great realm watching, under God's great
  frown!
Ever the same! The little children cleft
In twain: the little tender maidens reft
Of maidenhood! And through a little town
A stranger journeying, wrote this record
  down,
" In all the place there was not one man left."

O friend, the sudden lightning of whose pen

Makes Horror's countenance visible afar,

And Desolation's face familiar,

I think this very England of my ken

Is wondrous like that little town, where are

In all the streets and houses no more men.

XIX

STARVING ARMENIA

OPEN your hearts, ye clothed from head to
    feet,
Ye housed and whole who listen to the cry
Of them that not yet slain and mangled lie,
Only despoiled of all that made life sweet—
Only left bare to snow, and wind, and sleet,
And roofless to the inhospitable sky.
Give them of your abundance, lest they die,
And famine make this mighty woe com-
    plete ;
And lest—if truly, as your creeds aver,

A day of reckoning come—it be your lot

To hear the voice of the uprisen dead:

"We were the naked whom ye covered not,

The sick to whom ye did not minister,

Yea, and the hungry whom ye gave not

bread."

XX

TO THE SULTAN

Caliph, I did thee wrong. I hailed thee late
"Abdul the Damned," and would recall my
   word.
It merged thee with the unillustrious herd
Who crowd the approaches to the infernal
   gate—
Spirits gregarious, equal in their state
As is the innumerable ocean bird,
Gannet or gull, whose wandering plaint is
   heard
On Ailsa or Iona desolate.

For, in a world where cruel deeds abound,

The merely damned are legion : with such
souls

Is not each hollow and cranny of Tophet
crammed ?

Thou with the brightest of Hell's aureoles

Dost shine supreme, incomparably crowned,

Immortally, beyond all mortals, damned.

XXI

ON THE REPORTED EXPULSION OF AHMED RIZA BY THE FRENCH GOVERNMENT

WHEN, from supreme disaster, France uprose,

Shook her great wings and faced the world

   anew,

Who, if not we, rejoiced at heart to view

Her proud resilience after mightiest woes?

When 'neath the anarch's knife we saw the

   close

Of Carnot's day, amid her weepings who

Wept if not we, for the just man and true

That masked his strength in most urbane
  repose ?

And now again we mourn, but not with her,

Nay, not with her, though for her !—mourn
  to see

A tyrant, Hell's most perfect minister,

A man-fiend, sun him in her countenance ;

And Freedom, whose impassioned name was
  France,

Lie soiled and desecrate by France the Free.

XXII

ON A CERTAIN EUROPEAN
ALLIANCE

THE Hercules of nations, shaggy-browed,

Enormous-limbed, supreme on Steppe and
plain

Dwelt without consort, in his narrow brain

Nursing wide dreams he might not dream
aloud ;

Till him the radiant western Venus vowed

(So strange is love !) she pined for : and
these twain

Were wedded—Neptune, with his nereid-
   train,

Gracing the pageant of their nuptials proud.

Perfect in amorous arts, through eyes and
   ears

She fans her giant's not too fierce desire.

" How long, O Venus?   What impassioned
   years,

What ages of such rapture, ere thou tire? "

Thus the lewd gods : thus Mars and all his
   peers,

Gazing profane, at fault 'twixt mirth and ire.

XXIII

TO OUR SOVEREIGN LADY

QUEEN, that from Spring to Autumn of Thy
    reign
Hast taught Thy people how 'tis queenlier far
Than any golden pomp of peace or war,
Simply to be a woman without stain!
Queen whom we love, Who lovest us again!
We pray that yonder, by Thy wild Braemar,
The lord of many legions, the White Czar,
At this red hour, hath tarried not in vain.
We dream that from Thy words, perhaps
    Thy tears,

5

Ev'n in the King's inscrutable heart, shall
grow

Harvest of succour, weal, and gentler days!

So shall Thy lofty name to latest years

Still loftier sound, and ever sweetlier blow

The rose of Thy imperishable praise.

XXIV

THE AWAKENING

BEHOLD, she is risen who lay asleep so long,

Our England, our Belovèd! We have
    seen

The swelling of the waters, we have heard

The thundering cataracts call. Behold, she
    is risen,

Lovelier in resurrection than the face

Of vale or mountain, when, with storming
    tears,

At all Earth's portals knocks the impor-
    tunate Spring.

We watched her sleeping.   Day and
  night we strove
With the dread spell that drowsed her heart.
  And thrice
In the unrest of her sick dreams she stirred,
Half raised herself, half oped her lips and lids,
And thrice the evil charm prevailed, and
  thrice
She fell back forceless.   But behold, she is
  risen,
The Hope of the World is risen, is risen
  anew.

      O England ! O Belovèd ! O Re-born !
Look that thou fall not upon sleep again !
Thou art a star among the nations yet:

Be thou a light of succour unto them

That else are lost in blind and whelming

seas.

Around them is the tempest; over them,

Cold splendours of the inhospitable night,

Augustly unregardful : thou alone

Art still the North Star to the labouring

ship,

In friendless ocean the befriending orb,

And if thou shine not, whither is she steered?

Shine in thy glory, shine on her despair,

Shine lest she perish—lest of her no more

Than some lorn flotsam of mortality

Remain to catch the first auroral gleam,

When, in the East, flames the reluctant

dawn.

XXV

HOW WEARY IS OUR HEART

Of kings and courts; of kingly, courtly ways
In which the life of man is bought and
  sold ;
How weary is our heart these many days!

Of ceremonious embassies that hold
Parley with Hell in fine and silken phrase,
How weary is our heart these many days!

Of wavering counsellors neither hot nor
  cold,

Whom from His mouth God speweth, be it
    told
How weary is our heart these many days!

Yea, for the ravelled night is round the
    lands,
And sick are we of all the imperial story.
The tramp of Power, and its long trail of
    pain ;
The mighty brows in meanest arts grown
    hoary ;
The mighty hands,
That in the dear, affronted name of Peace
Bind down a people to be racked and slain ;
The emulous armies waxing without cease,
All-puissant all in vain ;

The pacts and leagues to murder by delays,

And the dumb throngs that on the deaf
thrones gaze ;

The common, loveless lust of territory ;

The lips that only babble of their mart,

While to the night the shrieking hamlets
blaze ;

The bought allegiance, and the purchased
praise,

False honour, and shameful glory ;—

Of all the evil whereof this is part,

How weary is our heart,

How weary is our heart these many days !

XXVI

EUROPE AT THE PLAY

O LANGUID audience, met to see

The last act of the tragedy

On that terrific stage afar,

Where burning towns the footlights are,—

O listless Europe, day by day

Callously sitting out the play!

So sat, with loveless count'nance cold,

Round the arena, Rome of old.

Pain, and the ebb of life's red tide,

So, with a calm regard, she eyed,

Her gorgeous vesture, million-pearled,

Splashed with the blood of half the world.

High was her glory's noon: as yet

She had not dreamed her sun could set!

As yet she had not dreamed how soon

Shadows should vex her glory's noon.

Another's pangs she counted nought;

Of human hearts she took no thought;

But God, at nightfall, in her ear

Thundered *His* thought exceeding clear.

Perchance in tempest and in blight,

On Europe, too, shall fall the night!

She sees the victim overborne,

By worse than ravening lions torn.

She sees, she hears, with soul unstirred,

And lifts no hand, and speaks no word,

But vaunts a brow like theirs who deem

Men's wrongs a phrase, men's rights a dream.

Yet haply she shall learn, too late,

In some blind hurricane of Fate,

How fierily alive the things

She held as fool's imaginings,

And, though circuitous and obscure,

The feet of Nemesis how sure.

www.ingramcontent.com/pod-product-compliance
Lightning Source LLC
Chambersburg PA
CBHW030022030726
47499CB00008B/3075